The BOATS on the RIVER

Story by
MARJORIE FLACK
Pictures by
JAY HYDE BARNUM

THE VIKING PRESS

VIKING
Published by the Penguin Group
Viking Penguin, a division of Penguin Books USA Inc.,
375 Hudson Street, New York, New York 10014, U.S.A.
Penguin Books Ltd, 27 Wrights Lane, London W8 5TZ, England
Penguin Books Australia Ltd, Ringwood, Victoria, Australia
Penguin Books Canada Ltd, 2801 John Street, Markham, Ontario, Canada L3R 1B4
Penguin Books (N.Z.) Ltd, 182–190 Wairau Road, Auckland 10, New Zealand

Penguin Books Ltd, Registered Offices: Harmondsworth, Middlesex, England

First published in 1946 by The Viking Press
Reissued 1991
1   3   5   7   9   10   8   6   4   2
Copyright Marjorie Flack Benet and Jay Hyde Barnum, 1946
Copyright renewed Norman von Rosenvinge, executor of the estate of Marjorie Flack Benet and
Hilma Barnum, 1974
All rights reserved

Library of Congress Catalog Card Number: 46-11852
ISBN: 0-670-83918-3

Printed in the United States of America

The river comes down from the mountains.
Down comes the river to the sea.
There are boats on the river.

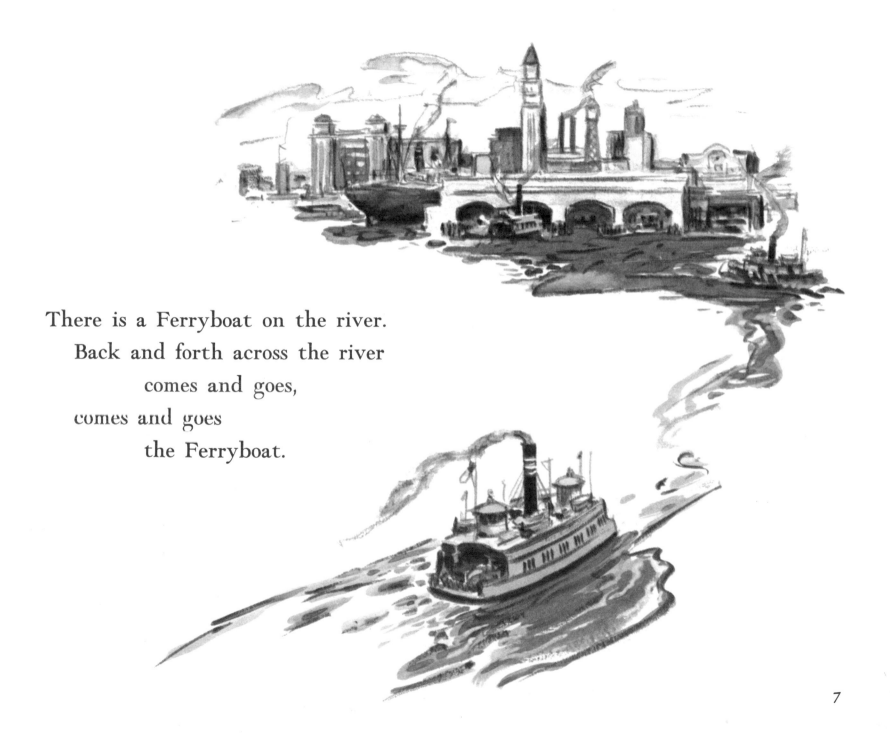

There is a Ferryboat on the river.
  Back and forth across the river
        comes and goes,
comes and goes
        the Ferryboat.

There is a Riverboat on the river,
a paddle-wheel Riverboat.
Up to the mountains,
down to the sea goes the Riverboat,
up and down, up and down.
Up and down the river
goes the Riverboat.

There is an Ocean Liner on the river;
an enormous Ocean Liner bringing
merchandise and people
and animals and letters
from the world across the ocean,
from Europe that is far across the sea.

There is a Tugboat on the river,
a busy Tugboat on the river,
busy, busy, busy, shoving,
pushing, pulling, tugging, helping
all the day.
The Tugboat helps the Ocean Liner,
and the Tugboat pulls the barges,
the barges full of coal,
full of coal to heat the houses
in the city near the sea.

There is a Motorboat on the river.
Quickly and swiftly hums the motor
of the Motorboat, speeding it over
the river.

There is a Sailboat on the river
and the Sailboat has no motor,
no motor to make it go;

but the wind blows in the white sail
and the Sailboat moves along, sails over the water.
This way and that way
goes the Sailboat with the wind.

There is a Rowboat on the river,
a tiny little Rowboat,
and the Rowboat has no motor,
the Rowboat has no sail.
A man with oars makes the Rowboat move,
rowing and rowing wherever he goes
wherever he goes on the river.

There is a Freightboat on the river.
  The Freightboat came from the tropics,
  came over the sea from the tropics.
  The Freightboat brings bananas
  to the children of the city,
  the city on the river
  near the sea.

There is a Submarine on the river.

The Submarine came up to float upon the river,

came up from underneath the sea,

to the top of the water from underneath the sea.

There is a Warship on the river,
a great American Warship.
There are sailors on the Warship.
The sailors come to visit in the city near the sea.

The sailors go
up the streets,

and down
the streets,

and visit
people's houses

The sailors go
in the stores,
and in the zoo,

and visit through the city,
through the city
on the river near the sea.

DO NOT FEED THE ANIMALS

Do the boats come to visit
in the city?
Do the boats go
up the streets,

and down the streets,
and visit people's houses?

Do the boats go
 in the stores, in the zoo,
 and visit through the city
 on the river near the sea?
No! The boats stay on the river,

the boats stay on the river
by the city near the sea.

When the Fog comes, comes in from the sea,
    all is gray in the city, all is gray on the river.
    Back and forth and up and down go the boats
    on the river in the Fog.
    "Whoooo!" call the big boats.
    "Whoooo–who–who!" calls the Tugboat,
    "Toot!" call the smaller boats,
calling each other every minute
every minute in the fog.

"Toot, toot, toot!" shouts the Sailboat,
"I am sailing, sailing before the wind.
Get out of my way—get out of my way!"
And all the big boats get out of her way
because the Sailboat
has no motor to make her go.

But the tiny little Rowboat
can not call or toot or whistle
so it hurries home to shore,
home away from all the boats
on the river in the Fog.

And when the night comes, it is dark over the sea,
dark over the city, dark over the river.
On each boat on the river are lights shining bright,
a red light on the left,
a green light on the right,
and a white light riding high.

There are lights on the Ferryboat, and on the Riverboat,
and on the Tugboat, and on the Ocean Liner,
and on the Sailboat and Motorboat, and on the Submarine.

There are lights on the Freightboat,
    and on the Warship.
There are lights on all the boats
    on the river,

the river that comes
from the mountains,
comes down
by the city
to the sea.

31